Paula
the Pumpkin
Fairy

Join the **Rainbow Magic Reading Challenge!**

Read the story and collect your fairy points to climb the

ok.

D0248181

To Lara and Isla, Happy Halloween!

ORCHARD BOOKS

First published in Great Britain in 2021 by The Watts Publishing Group

1 3 5 7 9 10 8 6 4 2

© 2021 Rainbow Magic Limited
© 2021 HIT Entertainment Limited
Illustrations © 2021 The Watts Publishing Group Limited

A CIP catalogue record for this book is available from the British Library.

ISBN 978 1 40836 451 2

Printed and bound in Great Britain by Clays Ltd, Elcograf S.p.A

MIX
Paper from
responsible sources
FSC® C104740

The paper and board used in this book are made from wood from responsible sources

Orchard Books
An imprint of Hachette Children's Group
Part of The Watts Publishing Group Limited
Carmelite House, 50 Victoria Embankment, London EC4Y 0DZ

An Hachette UK Company
www.hachette.co.uk
www.hachettechildrens.co.uk

Paula
the Pumpkin
Fairy

By Daisy Meadows

ORCHARD

www.orchardseriesbooks.co.uk

Contents

Story One:

The Spooky Jack-o'-lantern

Chapter One: Pumpkin Patch Farm   11
Chapter Two: Paula's Miniature Theatre   19
Chapter Three: A Hairy Thief   29
Chapter Four: Kirsty's Idea   39
Chapter Five: A Spooky Surprise   47

Story Two:
The Creepy Cookie

Chapter Six: A Pumpkin Carriage   61
Chapter Seven: Sawdust and Hot Water   69
Chapter Eight: A Pumpkin Passenger   77
Chapter Nine: Greedy Goblins   87
Chapter Ten: Good Dog!   97

Story Three:
The Petrifying Piñata

Chapter Eleven: Unwanted Guests   111
Chapter Twelve: Band-napped!   119
Chapter Thirteen: A Bad Ballroom   127
Chapter Fourteen: Hopping Mad   137
Chapter Fifteen: Happy Halloween, Jack Frost!   143

Jack Frost's Ode

Halloween's a time of year
That fills me up with spooky cheer.
My clever plot has now begun
To snatch the Pumpkin Fairy's fun.

Today will be a perfect day,
When everything will go my way.
With Paula's treats and decorations
I'll spoil all her celebrations!

Story One
The Spooky Jack-o'-lantern

Chapter One
Pumpkin Patch Farm

"This is the perfect place to spend Halloween," said Rachel Walker, looking around at the pumpkin field.

Rachel was staying with her best friend, Kirsty Tate, for the weekend. Kirsty's mum had just dropped them off for the Big Pumpkin Patch Pick at

Pumpkin Patch Farm on the outskirts of Wetherbury.

"We always manage to do something fun on Halloween," said Kirsty.

The girls shared a smile, remembering how they had met Trixie the Halloween Fairy and helped her to stop Jack Frost from spoiling the day for everyone. They had shared many magical adventures together, because the fairies often asked for their help when Jack Frost got up to mischief.

"I can't wait to pick our pumpkins," said Rachel. "I want to make the spookiest lantern ever."

The farmer was a friendly man in green wellies and a thick jumper. He grinned at the families who had gathered in the field.

"Good morning, and welcome to our first Big Pumpkin Patch Pick," he said. "My name is Peter Pine. There are lots of fun things to do here today, starting with finding your perfect pumpkin to carve.

They have been picked and lined up in rows. All you have to do is choose one!"

Kirsty knew many of the other children there, but she didn't recognise a tall, blonde girl who was standing apart from the other children. She had folded her arms and was scowling at the farmer.

"I wonder why she looks so cross," Rachel said.

"My mum says that sometimes, people who seem angry are actually really unhappy underneath," said Kirsty. "If we can get past her grumpiness, there's probably someone really lovely inside."

Rachel smiled.

"Let's try to make friends with her," she whispered.

"These beauties were planted at the beginning of June," Mr Pine continued. "Pumpkins take three or four months to grow, and that's why they're so ripe and orange now."

Kirsty stepped closer to the blonde girl and smiled at her.

"Hi," she said.

"Leave me alone," the girl mumbled.

"We only want to say hello," Kirsty went on. "This is Rachel and I'm Kirsty.

What's your name?"

"Polly," the girl said with a glare. "Now you've said hello, you can leave me alone."

As she turned away, Rachel saw tears glinting in her eyes.

"You're right," she said to Kirsty in a low voice. "I think she needs a friend."

She touched Polly's arm and tried again.

"Would you like to choose your pumpkin with us?" she asked.

"I hate pumpkins," Polly retorted.

16

"Oh," said Kirsty. "So, er, why have you come?"

"I had to," said Polly. "I live here. My dad bought this silly place and made me leave the city and come and live here."

"Wetherbury is lovely," said Kirsty. "I'm sure you'll like it if you give it a chance."

"Who owns that dog?" called out Mr Pine.

A little brown-and-white dog was scampering across the far end of the pumpkin patch. No one replied, but Rachel saw Polly staring at the animal until it disappeared into another field.

"Polly, could you help me?" called Mr Pine. "Some of the pumpkins seem to have gone missing."

Polly stomped off, muttering under her breath. Rachel and Kirsty started

walking along the row, looking at one round, ripe pumpkin after another.

"So Polly is homesick for her old life in the city," said Kirsty.

"It must be strange to move somewhere new and leave everything you know behind," said Rachel.

They reached the edge of the field and were about to turn around when they spotted something. Among the long grass, almost hidden from view, was a large pumpkin. Rachel and Kirsty waded into the tall grass to look at it.

"That's funny, it's already been carved," said Rachel.

Stars had been cut into the sides. Suddenly, a glowing light shone through the stars. Then the stalk lid wiggled . . . jiggled . . . and popped into the air!

Chapter Two
Paula's Miniature Theatre

Pumpkin-shaped sparkles burst into the air, and a tiny fairy fluttered out of the pumpkin. Her curly brown hair was gathered in two buns at the front, and hung in thick coils at the back. She was wearing a floaty purple dress with sleeves as gauzy as her wings, and orange pumpkins all around the hem.

"Hi," she said with a warm smile. "I'm
Paula the Pumpkin
Fairy, and I know
that you are Rachel
and Kirsty."

The girls tingled
from their toes to
their fingertips. It
was always exciting
to meet a new fairy.

"Welcome to
Wetherbury," said
Kirsty. "I love your
pumpkin dress."

"Thanks," said Paula, giving a little
twirl. "I love having a pumpkin pattern
on my clothes."

"It's great to meet you," said Rachel.

"Do you work with Trixie the Halloween
Fairy?"

"Oh yes, Trixie is my best friend," said
Paula. "We make sure that everything
about Halloween is a spooky success. It's
my job to create oodles of pumpkin fun
at parties."

"Have you come to check the
pumpkins here?" asked Rachel.

Paula's smile faded a little.

"No, I came to look for you," she said.
"Girls, I really need your help."

Rachel and Kirsty sat down in the long
grass, and Paula perched on Rachel's
knee.

"I grow pumpkins in a field next
to Trixie's Toadstool Cottage," Paula
explained. "Every year, at the Halloween
Harvest, all the fairies come together to

harvest the pumpkins and share them out. It's a lovely way to welcome in the autumn. But this year, Jack Frost demanded *all* the pumpkins for his Halloween Ball. When I refused . . ."

She waved her wand in a spiral. Fairy dust swirled towards the pumpkin and swooped in through one of the carved stars.

"Choose a star to peep through," said Paula.

Rachel and Kirsty lay down flat and each pressed one eye to a star. Inside the pumpkin was a moonlit field, where a tiny Paula and lots of other fairies were chatting and laughing as they placed pumpkins in wheelbarrows.

"It's like a miniature theatre," Kirsty whispered to Rachel.

The tiny Paula suddenly pointed to three goblins creeping along the far side of the field. Each one was carrying something that glowed purple in the twilight.

"They're stealing my magic!" Paula cried out.

As the fairies darted forwards, there was a loud *CRACK!* Jack Frost appeared, scowling, and the grass and the pumpkins crackled as they froze.

"If I can't have the pumpkins, then neither can you," he hissed. "I'll destroy your crop and steal all the pumpkins

from the human world."

There was a bright flash of blue lightning, and then the pumpkin theatre went dark.

"Oh my goodness, what did the goblins steal?" asked Kirsty, sitting up.

"The three extra-magical objects

that help me to do my job," said Paula. "Without them, I can't stop him."

"We'll help," said Rachel. "We'll do it together."

"That's what I hoped you would say," Paula said, bouncing up and down in excitement.

"Tell us about what's been taken," said Kirsty.

"The spooky jack-o'-lantern makes sure that there are enough pumpkins for carving decorations for Halloween," Paula said. "The creepy cookie helps people make yummy pumpkin treat, and the petrifying piñata makes sure that there are plenty of games and fun to be had at Halloween."

"They sound really special," said Rachel, smiling.

"They even have a magical purple glow so they're easy to spot," said Paula. "Purple is one of my favourite colours."

Just then, Mr Pine's voice rang out across the field.

"It's time to start carving," he called. "Bring your pumpkins to the barn and let's make some lanterns."

Chapter Three
A Hairy Thief

Paula hid in the hood of Rachel's jumper
and the girls headed down to the barn.
They meant to choose their pumpkins on
the way, but there was none left.

A live band called The Harvesters
were playing inside the barn, and a few
people had started to dance. Others were

standing around tables, waiting to carve their pumpkins.

"Why haven't they started?" Rachel wondered.

Mr Pine looked puzzled. He searched through a box filled with paint, glitter, glue and stickers, but there were no tools.

"I bought lots of them at the craft shop," he said. "Where could they have gone? Boys, do you have any carving tools?"

A group of boys was huddling around a table near the barn door, half hidden

under bobble hats, scarves and ponchos. Their table was already filled with amazing jack-o'-lanterns with all sorts of expressions. Some of them were playing with the patterns that the farmer had printed out. More patterns had fallen on the ground. The boys were trampling all over them in their large green wellies.

"No, leave us alone," they retorted.

Rachel and Kirsty gasped and shared a surprised glance.

"Strange boys with big feet and bad manners," said Rachel. "I think they could be goblins!"

At that moment, The Harvesters finished their song and everyone clapped. The boys jumped and scowled at the sudden noise. Among the carved pumpkins on the table, Rachel suddenly glimpsed a small jack-o'-lantern with a sparkly purple glow.

"I think that's Paula's lantern," she cried. "They *are* goblins!"

Just then, everything seemed to happen at once. The goblins heard Rachel and whirled around. The Harvesters started playing their next song, and the brown-

and-white stray dog ran into the barn.

"Go away!" squawked the goblins.

BOOM BA-DA BOOM went the drums.

WOOF! barked the dog. She took a flying leap at the table, seized the little lantern in her jaws, and ran out of the barn at full pelt!

"Stop that hairy thief!" yelled the goblins.

They ran after the dog, but someone else was ahead of them. To the girls' surprise, Polly was chasing the little stray.

"We have to save the lantern," cried Kirsty. "Hurry!"

A Hairy Thief

They raced after Polly and the goblins. Paula bounced up and down in Rachel's hood, clinging on tightly and laughing helplessly.

"This is better than a fairground ride," she shouted. "Woohoo!"

The dog scampered up to the end of the field and stopped. Polly stopped too. She knelt down and gently held out her hand. The dog wagged her tail and took a step forward. But then the goblins charged towards her, yelling. The dog zigzagged around them, swerved away from the girls and ran through one of the goblins' legs. He let out a surprised squawk and the dog yelped.

"You're scaring her!" cried Polly.

She tripped and fell down. Rachel and Kirsty ran to help her, and the dog

disappeared into the next field, followed by the goblins.

"Oh my goodness, are you OK?" asked Kirsty.

Polly rubbed her ankle.

"I think I've sprained it," she said.

Tears spilled down her cheeks, and the girls put their arms around her.

"Poor you, it must be really painful," said Rachel.

"That's not why I'm crying," said Polly in a fierce voice. "I just can't stop thinking about how much I miss my home."

Rachel and Kirsty felt sorry for her.

"I can imagine it must be scary to leave everything you know behind," said Kirsty gently. "Wetherbury is a lovely place too. I'll help you to see all the good things about it. But first we have to get you back to the barn."

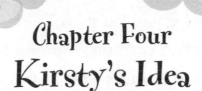

Chapter Four
Kirsty's Idea

Between them, the girls helped Polly to limp down the field to the barn. When Mr Pine heard what had happened, he fetched some ice for her ankle and gave her a big cuddle. She leaned on his shoulder.

"What are we going to do now?" asked

Rachel in a quiet voice. "The dog got away and so did the goblins. They could be five fields away by now."

Kirsty looked around. No one had started carving, and some of the other children were looking bored. A few more visitors had arrived, but there didn't seem to be enough pumpkins to go around. People looked disappointed and annoyed.

"Mr Pine's open day isn't going very well," said Kirsty.

"It's because my lantern is missing," said Paula. "Everything to do with carving pumpkins for decorations is all mixed up. Until I get it back, there won't be enough pumpkins for carving, lanterns won't look good and Halloween parties won't have the right decorations."

Just then, the goblins swaggered back

into the barn, carrying the spooky jack-
o'-lantern.

"The dog must have dropped it," said
Rachel. "We have to think of a way to
get it back."

Paula

"I'll zoom over there and *make* them give it to me," exclaimed Paula, peeking out from Rachel's hood. "I won't let Halloween be a disaster because of them!"

"Paula, you can't," Kirsty whispered. "Someone is bound to see you."

The goblins were complaining.

"I don't like this place," said a goblin in a blue bobble hat. "I want to go home."

"Yeah," said a goblin in a yellow scarf. "There are no hairy, panting animals with enormous teeth and long pink tongues in Goblin Grotto."

"You know Jack Frost's orders," snapped the tallest goblin, whose nose had gone red. "We have to keep the lantern away from Fairyland and decorate lots of pumpkins for his ball. Even if we went

42

back to the castle, he'd only yell more orders at us."

"*Humph*," said the goblin in the blue bobble hat. "The Ice Castle is the only place worse than this boring pumpkin farm and that horrible, hairy animal."

The Harvesters had just finished a song, so the goblin's last words rang out loudly.

"Hey, don't be so rude," said Polly, turning in her chair and glaring at him. "My dad has worked really hard on this farm. Besides, the dog was only playing. You shouldn't be such scaredy-cats."

"We're not scared," the goblin retorted. "And we're not staying here to be insulted."

The goblins stormed out, and Mr Pine groaned.

"Thanks for standing up for me, love,"

he said to Polly. "But I'm afraid I'm disappointing all our visitors. Without the carving tools, our first pumpkin day is going to be a giant flop."

The girls felt awful. They knew why the tools and pumpkins had gone missing.

"It's so unfair that Jack Frost is spoiling things for everyone here," said Rachel. "Especially Polly and her dad."

Suddenly, Kirsty had an idea. Impulsively, she climbed up on to a bale of hay and spoke in her loudest voice.

"Ladies and gentlemen, carving pumpkins is lots of fun," she said. "But maybe this year, you could try something different. There are other ways of decorating pumpkins. Mr Pine has an amazing craft box full of possibilities. You could paint a pumpkin white and then

paint an autumn scene on it."

"Yes," said Rachel, jumping up beside her best friend. "You could stencil leaf shapes on a pumpkin and colour them with glitter."

"Or use stick-on jewels to make spooky faces," Kirsty went on.

"These girls are right," said Mr Pine, lifting the craft box on to a table. "Please come and help yourselves."

People started to come forward, talking about their ideas. Mr Pine beamed at the girls as they jumped down from the hay bale.

"Thank you," he said. "That gives me a bit of time to search for the missing tools – and the pumpkins!"

"And it gives *us* time to find the goblins," said Rachel under her breath.

Chapter Five
A Spooky Surprise

The girls went outside. There was no one in the pumpkin field, so they walked around the back of the barn. The grass was long and overgrown, but they could hear giggling coming from within.

"I can't bear to hide any more," said Paula, darting out of Rachel's hood

and hovering above them. "I have to do something!"

"Can you see anyone in the long grass?" Rachel whispered.

Paula looked down and nodded.

"It's the goblins," she exclaimed. "They've got all Mr Pine's missing pumpkins!"

Rachel and Kirsty pushed their way

through the long grass, with Paula flying above to guide them. They could hear the goblins squawking with laughter. Soon they reached a clearing where the grass had been flattened down. The goblins were there with a pile of stolen pumpkins. They were stamping their feet into them to turn them into silly shoes.

Paula swooped towards them.

"Yikes, a fairy!" cried the goblin in the blue bobble hat.

"And those interfering humans," added a goblin in a stripy poncho. "Go away!"

"Give those pumpkins back," said Paula. "You're spoiling them before they have a chance to be part of Halloween."

"You can't stop us," said the goblin carrying the lantern.

He rolled a pumpkin towards Rachel and Kirsty like a bowling ball. They dived sideways, and he cackled with laughter.

The little Pumpkin Fairy looked as if she might burst into tears. But before she could say anything, the goblin went pale and pointed into the long grass.

"Wh-wh-what's th-th-that?" he stammered.

A spooky orange head was rising out of the long grass, with wide eyes and an even wider mouth. Kirsty and Rachel gasped.

"It's alive!" the goblins squealed in fright.

They turned and ran, dropping their hats and scarves as they went. The lantern fell to the ground too.

"What is it?" whispered Rachel, feeling the hairs on her arms stand up.

The carved pumpkin wobbled and then dropped on to the grass. Underneath was the little brown-and-white dog.

WOOF! she said, with her mouth open as if she were laughing.

Kirsty and Rachel let out their breath

as the dog ran to pick up Paula's magical lantern. She looked up at Paula, and then put it carefully down in front of her.

"Thank you," said Paula, smiling.

She swooped down and touched the lantern, which instantly returned to fairy size. The girls stepped forward to stroke the dog, but she scampered away.

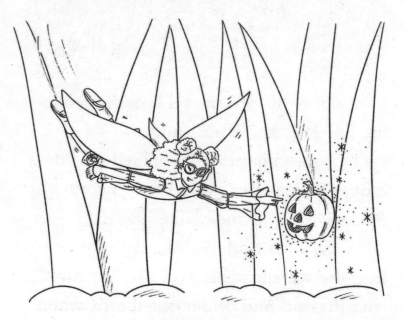

"We did it," said Paula. "Thank you, girls. For a minute there I thought a pumpkin really had come to life!"

"Me too," said Rachel, giggling.

"I guess Halloween is supposed to be a bit scary," Kirsty added with a laugh. "Paula, will everything be OK for Mr Pine now?"

"As soon as I'm back in Fairyland, he will find his tools," said Paula. "And you can tell him where to find his missing pumpkins."

Holding her lantern tightly, she disappeared in a whoosh of sparkling fairy dust.

"Now we just have two more objects to find," said Rachel. "Let's go and tell Mr Pine the good news about his pumpkins!"

Story Two
The Creepy Cookie

Chapter Six
A Pumpkin Carriage

After they had carved their pumpkins,
Rachel and Kirsty ate their lunch
on a hay bale outside the barn. The
Harvesters' music was soothing, and
the autumn sunshine made them feel
enjoyably sleepy.

"My fingers are aching after all that

carving," said Rachel with a yawn.

Kirsty looked around at the other visitors who were picnicking on the hay bales.

"I wonder where Polly has gone," she said.

The girls found the farmer's daughter inside the barn. All the carved pumpkins

were on display in the darkest corner. Each one had been completed with a candle, and a flickering, spooky glow was dancing across the barn walls. Polly was sitting at the carving table, and she turned when she heard Kirsty's voice.

"Hi, Polly," said Rachel. "How's your ankle feeling?"

"It's still a bit sore," Polly replied. "Carving this took my mind off it, though."

The girls gasped when they saw her lantern. She had coiled and twisted gold-coloured wire to turn the pumpkin into Cinderella's carriage. Tiny windows were cut into the sides, and there was a little door decorated with gold sequins.

"That's beautiful, Polly," said Kirsty.

"You're really talented."

Polly flushed but looked pleased, and soon, several people had gathered around to admire her creation.

"This is the first thing I've enjoyed since I came to Wetherbury," she said.

"Maybe you could learn to like it here after all," said Rachel.

A boy called Joseph passed by.

"Don't forget that everyone is invited to our Halloween party," he called out.

"It's brilliant fun," said Kirsty. "Joseph's family has a party every

year. There are always lots of games and
yummy Halloween food."

"I'd love to come," said Polly. "Last
year, the games at my friend Hazel's
party were so much fun . . ."

Her lips trembled, and Kirsty squeezed
her shoulders.

"Are you missing your friend?" she said.

"I'm worried that she'll forget about
me," said Polly in a low voice.

Rachel and Kirsty shared a determined
glance. Paula wasn't the only one who
needed their help.

Rachel sat down beside Polly.

"Kirsty and I don't see each other all
the time," she said. "We don't go to the
same school. But that doesn't stop us from
being best friends, and I bet it won't stop
you and Hazel either."

"Have you told your dad how you feel?" asked Kirsty.

Polly shook her head.

"He's been so excited about the farm," she said with a shrug. "I don't want to upset him."

Rachel pulled Kirsty aside.

"I've got an idea," she said. "Let's tell Mr Pine that Polly's missing her friend. He might invite her for a visit."

Chapter Seven
Sawdust and Hot Water

As soon as he heard how Polly was
feeling, Mr Pine promised to invite Hazel
the very next weekend. But he broke off
as he was telling Polly the good news,
and stared at a visitor who had just come
into the barn.

Rachel and Kirsty saw a woman with

spiky silver hair
and a swirling
purple coat.
An expensive-
looking camera
hung over her
shoulder.

"Do you know
who that is?" Mr
Pine whispered in an
excited voice. "That's Ursula Pring. She
writes for the local newspaper."

"Do you think she's here to write
about the farm?" asked Polly.

"I hope so," said Mr Pine. "If she
praises it, people will come to buy our
pumpkins. Maybe we could even think
about opening a farm shop. But I can't
tell her about the amazing food yet. I

still have to show the visitors around the
Pumpkin Experience."

"I'll do that, Dad," said Polly. "You
concentrate on showing her the food stall.
This is our big chance."

"What's the Pumpkin Experience?" asked Kirsty as Mr Pine hurried back to the food stall.

"It was Dad's idea," said Polly. "It's a place where visitors can discover all the things they can do with pumpkins. There's more to pumpkins than jack-o'-lanterns, you know."

Rachel laughed.

"You almost sound as if you like them," she said.

"Maybe," said Polly with a sudden grin. "Just a *little* bit more than before."

She turned to the visitors who were starting to gather nearby.

"Ladies and gentlemen, it's time for me to show you that there is more to pumpkins than meets the eye," she said.

Polly led the visitors away, and the girls

went to see Mr Pine's food stall. A queue of people had already lined up in front of his display of pumpkin pasties, soup and pasta, but he looked worried. A couple of teenage girls walked away past Rachel and Kirsty.

"Yuck, this pasty tastes like sawdust," said one, throwing it into a bin.

"The soup is just like hot water," said the other, curling her lip.

"Are you sure you've grown the right *sort* of pumpkins?" asked a man in a flat cap.

The girls shared a worried glance.

"Did you hear that?" Rachel asked in a low voice. "People are starting to wonder if Mr Pine knows what he's doing."

"And the food tastes horrid," added Kirsty, biting her lip in worry. "This must be happening because the creepy cookie is missing."

Paula had told

74

them that the creepy cookie helped
people make yummy pumpkin treats for
Halloween. Without it, food made with
pumpkins was bound to go wrong.

Rachel looked around, looking for
Ursula Pring. Then she suddenly grabbed
Kirsty's hand and pulled her back
towards the pumpkin-carving table.

"Look at Polly's pumpkin carriage," she
whispered, pointing to the carving table.

The coiled gold and sequins were glowing, and light was coming from inside the carriage. Kirsty felt Rachel's hand trembling with excitement.

"Polly didn't add a candle," she said. "So where's that light coming from?"

The girls shared a secret smile.

"Magic," they whispered.

Chapter Eight
A Pumpkin Passenger

The carriage door opened, and Paula stepped out, beaming at them.

"Best way to travel ever," she said, looking around. "Wow, something smells good."

"If only it *tasted* good," said Kirsty, holding open her pocket. "Everyone is

complaining about the food, and there's a reporter here from the local paper. If she writes about the food being horrible, no one will want to visit."

"It could ruin Mr Pine's farm," said Rachel. "It's really good to see you, Paula."

Paula fluttered into Kirsty's pocket. The girls were blocking people's view of the carriage, but they couldn't risk Paula being seen.

As they walked past the food stall, they saw that the queue had vanished.

"Yum, are those pumpkin pasties?" asked Paula, popping her head out of the pocket.

"You really have to stay out of sight," said Rachel.

"Sorry," said Paula. "It's just that I love thinking up new scrumptious pumpkin recipes. You can boil them, steam them, roast them and mash them. They're even used as medicine in some places around the world."

She ducked back inside the pocket and the girls leaned against a wall as if they were talking to each other.

"I can't bear for humans to think this amazing vegetable tastes bad," Paula continued in a muffled voice. "I wish you could have been at some of our

Halloween feasts. I've even cooked pumpkin leaves before. The trick is to boil them first and then—"

"Paula, please, we have to concentrate on finding the creepy cookie," said Rachel. "Without it, the reporter will write that the food here tastes awful, and no one will come to buy the pumpkins."

"Sorry," said Paula again. "I get carried away when I'm talking about pumpkins! How are we going to keep that reporter away from the food?"

"You two could look for the goblins and the creepy cookie while I show her around the Pumpkin Experience," Rachel suggested.

"Yes, let's try that," said Paula. "Remember, the cookie glows purple so it's easy to spot."

"Good luck," said Kirsty to Rachel. "We'll find the goblins as quickly as we can."

Kirsty ducked out of sight behind a wheelbarrow filled with pumpkins. Rachel spotted Ursula's purple coat heading towards the food stall. She darted forwards and stood in front of her, blocking her way.

"Hi, Ms Pring," she said, smiling. "My name's Rachel and I'm going to show you around. Do you like music?"

"Oh, I . . . er . . ." said Ursula, looking confused and surprised.

Rachel took her arm and led her towards The Harvesters.

"Hurry up, Kirsty and Paula," she murmured under her breath.

"Er . . . I actually came to try the food and drink," said Ursula. "Thanks for showing me the band but I really should be going."

She started to move back towards the food stall. Rachel gulped and leapt after her.

"You have to see the Pumpkin Experience," she said, grabbing Ursula's hand and pulling her away. "It's such an important part of the day."

On the far side of the barn, Polly
was showing some younger children
how to make pumpkin-seed necklaces.
Rachel could see a face-painting stall, a
headdress-making table and a 'guess the
number of seeds in the jar' competition.

*I just hope this is enough to keep Ursula
Pring away from the food*, she thought.

Chapter Nine
Greedy Goblins

Meanwhile, behind the wheelbarrow, Paula was also thinking about food.

"There's pumpkin hummus, pumpkin lasagne, pumpkin ice cream—" she was saying, counting the dishes off on her fingers.

"Paula, Rachel can't keep the reporter

away from the food for ever," said Kirsty
in an urgent voice. "Why don't you
turn me into a fairy? We'd have a better
chance of spotting the goblins that way."

"Yes, good plan," said Paula.

She raised her
wand and a
round, orange
shape appeared at
the tip, growing
quickly into
a miniature
pumpkin. Paula
flicked her wand
towards Kirsty,
and the little
pumpkin bounced
through the air
towards her and

burst above her head. Instead of pumpkin seeds, glittering fairy dust cascaded down on her. Kirsty felt her body shrinking to fairy size. Then the sparkles cleared and she was fluttering in the air beside Paula, with wings like pearly gauze. Suddenly the pumpkins in the wheelbarrow looked gigantic.

"Let's check outside first," said Paula.

Back at the Pumpkin Experience, Rachel had persuaded Ursula to have her face painted. Her gaze wandered to a small crowd of children wearing blue capes. They had crowded around something on a table. Feeling curious, Rachel peered over their shoulders. The children were snatching sweets out of a

jar labelled 'Sweet Prizes. Do Not Touch.'
They were stuffing sweets, chocolate
bars and candy canes into their trick-or-
treat baskets. Bonbons, lemon sherbets,
humbugs and fizzy cola bottles were
spilling to the floor.

"Hey, wait," Rachel exclaimed. "That
jar is for prizes. I don't think you're

supposed to be—"

The children whirled around. Each had the same horribly familiar face, with a cruel mouth, a long nose and cold, hard eyes.

"Jack Frost," Rachel said with a gasp. "But how?"

Her heart thudded, and then she understood.

"Those are masks," she said in a shocked whisper. "You're goblins!"

"These are for Jack Frost's Halloween ball," snapped the biggest goblin. "Anyway, it's none of your business. Shut up and go away."

"That's very rude," said Rachel, looking down at their baskets and the mess they had made. "These sweets are . . ."

Her voice trailed off because she had noticed something that pushed all other thoughts out of her mind. Inside one of the baskets was a large purple cookie.

Rachel glanced at Ursula. Her eyes were shut and her face paint was only half finished. There was still time to find Kirsty and Paula. Rachel raced through the barn, looking up and all around for her friends. The light was already fading, and at first there was no sign of them. She ran outside and behind the barn, where they had found the goblins earlier. There she saw the stray dog, wagging her tail. Kirsty and Paula were hovering in front of her.

"We just want to make friends and ask if you've seen any goblins," Kirsty was saying.

The dog stuck out her tongue and panted. Kirsty laughed.

"You're cute," she said, "but you're not very helpful."

"I've found them all," Rachel called out. "The goblins *and* the creepy cookie."

With a bark of alarm, the dog turned and ran away. Paula flicked her wand at Rachel, who shrank to fairy size in a flurry of orange sparkles.

"Time to rescue my cookie," Paula cheered.

Chapter Ten
Good Dog!

Inside the barn, the fairies saw the goblins swaggering through the crowd with their overflowing baskets. They kept bumping into people on purpose and shouting "BOO!" at babies.

"Oh no you don't," muttered Paula, her cheeks going pink. "I'm putting a stop to

that right now."

"Wait!" cried
Rachel.

But Paula
zoomed towards
the goblins like
an arrow. Mr Pine
was striding towards
them too.

"She'll bump into him," cried Kirsty.
"Come on!"

They darted after her.

"Stop this at once," Mr Pine called out.
"You are frightening people."

Rachel and Kirsty yanked Paula aside
and they shot into the basket of the
shortest goblin. Terrified by the sudden
bump, he screamed and flung the basket
into the air. The other goblins panicked

immediately. Sweets, chocolate bars,
fairies and the precious cookie went
soaring into the air.

"Let's get out of here!" squawked the biggest goblin.

They stampeded out of the barn as Rachel, Kirsty and Paula fluttered down behind a hay bale. With a wave of Paula's wand, the girls were human again.

"Paula, hide in my pocket," said Kirsty, panting. "We have to find that cookie."

They scrambled out from behind the hay bale and groaned. Every visitor on the farm was helping to pick up the sweets. Someone had placed the jar on a table, and it was quickly filling up again.

"For once, I wish people weren't so eager to help," said Rachel, scanning the straw-covered ground.

"Over there!" Kirsty exclaimed.

Something was glowing
purple beside the
apple-bobbing
game. The girls
weaved their way
through the crowd
towards it, but
they were too slow.
In dismay, they saw

Polly pick up the cookie and drop it into
the jar.

"Take it," Paula urged them.

"We can't," said Kirsty with a groan.
"People would think we were stealing."

Mr Pine walked towards the jar,
carrying the lid. Rachel buried her face
in her hands.

"We've failed," she said.

WOOF!

Rachel looked up.

WOOF! WOOF!

The crowd parted as the little brown-and-white dog came charging through the barn.

"Everyone's looking at the dog," Kirsty whispered, standing in front of the jar. "Paula, this is your chance."

Paula swooped into the jar so fast that she was a blur. As soon as she touched the glowing cookie, it shrank to fairy size.

"Thank goodness for that dog," said Rachel. "She's saved us again."

"I'll see you soon," Paula whispered.

Rachel and Kirsty turned to look at the jar, but Paula had already disappeared back to Fairyland. The girls shared a relieved smile and collapsed on to a hay bale.

"Now Ursula can try as much food as she likes," said Kirsty. "It will be completely delicious."

"And there's only one magical object left to find," Rachel added.

"Yes, but we have to find it quickly," said Kirsty. "Without the petrifying piñata, Halloween party fun won't happen!"

Story Three
The Petrifying Piñata

Chapter Eleven
Unwanted Guests

"Flying really works up an appetite," said Rachel, before taking a huge bite of a pumpkin pasty. "Mmm, this is scrummy."

Kirsty tried the pumpkin soup and licked her lips.

"This is the tastiest soup I've ever had," she said, smiling. "Thank goodness we

found the creepy cookie."

The journalist Ursula Pring was also trying some pumpkin treats from Mr Pine's food stall.

"Delicious," she exclaimed. "I must get some photos for my article."

The girls exchanged a happy smile.

"It sounds as if Pumpkin Patch Farm is going to get a good write-up in the local paper," said Rachel.

"Brilliant," said Kirsty. "Now all we have to do is find the petrifying piñata and everything will be – oh dear."

She broke off and stared across the barn at her friend Joseph. He was talking to his parents. They looked worried, and Joseph seemed upset. The girls saw him wipe his eyes on his sleeve.

"Something's wrong," said Rachel. "Let's try to help."

As they walked over, Joseph saw them and came to meet them.

"Our Halloween party is cancelled," he said in a miserable

voice. "There's a gas leak in the village hall, so we can't use it."

"Isn't there anywhere else you could use?" Rachel asked.

"It's too late," said Joseph, sniffing. "The community hall is booked and the Playhouse Theatre has a special Halloween show. Even the warehouse is busy."

"I guess Halloween is a popular night for parties," said Polly, who was standing nearby. "But you . . . you could use this barn."

Joseph gasped.

"Really?" he asked.

"I'll ask my dad," Polly said. "I'm sure he'll say yes."

She ran over to Mr Pine, who smiled and nodded as she explained. Then Polly

turned and gave
them the thumbs up.

"Yes!" said Joseph
and he ran to tell
his parents the
good news.

Joseph's dad
went to fetch the
decorations. His
mum phoned the
guests to tell them
where the party
would be held.

"I'll clear a space for the party games,"
said Polly.

Joseph and Kirsty started tidying up,
while Rachel went to ask the band if
they could stay for a while longer and
play some party music.

"We'd be happy to," said the lead singer of The Harvesters. "We love Halloween parties!"

Soon, Joseph's dad was back with two boxes. The first box was brimming with decorations. The children hung paper bats from the ceiling, draped everything in fake cobwebs and placed grinning, candlelit pumpkins all around the barn.

"I can't wait to play the games," Joseph said to Polly as they hung the skeleton garlands. "My favourite is the piñata."

Rachel and Kirsty exchanged a worried glance. They still hadn't found Paula's missing piñata. Without its special magic, all the Halloween games would go wrong.

Soon, the barn was looking very creepy. The Harvesters were playing a spooky song, and the first guests looked around in wonder as they came in. As Rachel and Kirsty looked at all the cool costumes, a group of boys arrived in swirling capes and ghost masks.

"Wow, they look brilliant," said Rachel.

But her smile faded when someone horribly familiar stepped out from behind the boys. *Jack Frost!*

Chapter Twelve
Band-napped!

Jack Frost swaggered into the barn,
sneering at the people who were already
dancing to the music. An icy mist swirled
at his feet, and the air grew colder.

"Look at those silly humans," he hissed.
"Perhaps I'll take their band for my
Halloween Ball and spoil their fun."

"He *can't*," said Kirsty in alarm.

"What would happen if he took grown-ups to Fairyland?" Rachel asked.

"I don't know," Kirsty replied, feeling worried.

At that moment, Joseph's dad let out an exclamation. He had opened the second box and lifted out a carton labelled 'apple bobbing'.

"That's funny," he said, frowning. "There are no apples in here."

"That's the 'pin the stalk on the pumpkin' game," said Joseph, pointing to a large envelope.

Polly opened the envelope and shook her head.

"It's empty," she said.

One by one, the games were unpacked. Each one had a problem. The 'guess the weight of the pumpkin' game was missing the scales. There was only one toilet roll for the toilet-paper-mummy challenge.

"This piñata looks OK," said Joseph's dad.

Rachel and Kirsty shared a hopeful glance. Could Paula's magical pumpkin-shaped piñata be hiding in the box of games? But they sighed when they saw that it was in the shape of a witch's hat. Joseph's dad hung it from a rafter.

"Who wants to go first?" he asked.

Giggling, Polly whacked the piñata with an old broom handle. At once, the string broke and the piñata dropped to the ground. It burst open, but nothing spilled out. The children knelt down to look at it.

"Where are all the sweets?" asked Polly.

Just then, Rachel heard a squawk of surprise behind her.

"So *that's* what that weird pumpkin thing is," said a greedy voice. "It's got sweets inside it."

She peeped over her shoulder. Two goblins were standing nearby, disguised in their swirling cloaks and ghost masks. They hadn't noticed her.

"We should bash it, and see what comes out," said the second goblin. "Come on."

The goblins scurried away.

"Kirsty, do you think they're talking about Paula's piñata?" whispered Rachel.

Kirsty jumped to her feet and pulled Rachel up beside her.

"Let's follow them," she said.

As they weaved between the chatting guests, they saw The Harvesters heading

123

out of the barn.

"They're taking a break," Kirsty said. "Look!"

Jack Frost was creeping out of the barn behind them.

Rachel and Kirsty slipped outside and ducked down behind some bales of straw in the moonlight. The band was chatting as they gazed up at the moon. Bare trees stretched their branches towards the sky like bony goblin hands. Jack Frost was lurking a little way behind them.

"Great night for a Halloween party," said the lead singer, rubbing his hands together. "Let's think of a few more spooky songs that we can play."

A sneer twisted Jack Frost's face. He raised his wand and pointed it at The Harvesters. There was a dazzling flash of blue lightning, and the girls covered their eyes. When they peeped through their fingers, Jack Frost had disappeared . . . and so had The Harvesters!

Chapter Thirteen
A Bad Ballroom

Kirsty fumbled for the locket around her neck.

"We have to follow them," she said.

Queen Titania had given them the necklaces with just enough fairy dust to carry them to Fairyland. Rachel's fingers trembled as she opened her locket.

"Take us to Jack Frost's Castle," she said, sprinkling the fairy dust over her head.

"And please bring Paula to meet us there," added Kirsty quickly, doing the same with her fairy dust.

There was a whooshing sound, and the distant tinkle of silver bells, and Pumpkin Patch Farm disappeared. The girls spun and twirled in a haze of sparkles. *WHUMP!* They landed in something white, powdery and cold.

"Snowdrift," said Kirsty, spluttering and wiping snow from her face.

"At least it was a soft landing," said Rachel.

They were close to the Ice Castle. A snow cloud hung low over the tip of the tallest tower, like white-grey candy floss wrapped around an icicle.

Rachel and Kirsty shook snow from their glimmering fairy wings and rubbed their arms, trying to get warm. Seconds later, there was another *WHUMP!* and Paula fell into the snowdrift.

"Hello," she exclaimed, beaming up at them. "Goodness, that was a surprise! I was just about to tuck into a pumpkin muffin. Have you ever tried one? The secret is the gingerbread-flavoured icing, and I always add a pinch of – oh my word! Is that Jack Frost's Castle?"

Rachel and Kirsty pulled her out of the snowdrift.

"Paula, we can't talk about pumpkin recipes right now," said Kirsty in an urgent voice. "Jack Frost has brought the musicians from the party here to play at his ball."

"We have to rescue them," said Rachel. "But how are we going to get in?"

Paula waved her wand and drew a cylinder shape in the air, made of pumpkin-shaped sparkles. The sparkles

pressed themselves together to form a tiny orange telescope. She plucked it out of the air and held it to one eye.

"We can just walk straight in," she said, passing the telescope to Rachel and then Kirsty.

They looked through it in turn. The castle doors were wide open and there were several mouldy pumpkins standing by the entrance. Balls of cotton wool had been stapled to the door, and on a scrap of paper were scrawled the words 'Welcome to the Halloween Ball'.

Paula waved her wand again, and
the fairies were wrapped in thick, black
cloaks. Each of them was wearing a Jack
Frost mask, just like the goblins in the
barn.

"Brilliant,"
said Kirsty
with a giggle.
"They'll think
we're goblins
dressed up for
Halloween."

No one
stopped them
from walking inside. They could hear
shouting, and they tiptoed along a dark
corridor until they reached a set of half-
open double doors. The shouting was
coming from inside.

"The cotton wool doesn't look anything like spiders' webs," Jack Frost was ranting. "Why are all my pumpkins mouldy? Where is the party food?"

The fairies peeped inside. They saw a vast ballroom, but it didn't look ready for a ball. The dance floor was marked with smears and footprints. The curtains were tattered, and the only decoration was a clump of cotton wool that had been glued to the ceiling.

Jack Frost was standing in front of three goblins, who were bowing so low that their long noses were scraping on the ground.

"We did our best, Your Iciness," one of the goblins wailed. "We need the magical jack-o'-lantern and cookie."

"Then you shouldn't have let those

pesky humans take them!" Jack Frost bawled. "This place is supposed to look spooky!"

Rachel glanced into a far corner of the drab ballroom and gasped. The Harvesters were lying on the floor, their eyes shut.

Chapter Fourteen
Hopping Mad

"What has he done to the band?" asked Kirsty in alarm.

"Don't worry, they're just asleep," said Paula. "The journey to Fairyland is too hard for grown-ups. They won't wake up until they are back in the human world."

"Can you magic them back home?"

Rachel asked.

"Yes, but I need to be closer to them," said Paula.

"We'll distract Jack Frost," said Kirsty.

Bravely, she and Rachel hurried into the room. Jack Frost glared at them.

"Well?" he snapped.

"We could put on a show to entertain the guests," said Kirsty in a squawky voice.

She and Rachel started to jump and hop around, waving their hands in the air. Jack Frost's mouth fell open.

"Have you gone loopy?' he demanded.

Behind him, Paula waved her wand over The Harvesters. They melted away as if they had never been there. Then she joined in with Rachel and Kirsty.

Jack Frost was purple with fury.

"Stop!" he screeched. "Stop hopping around like mad frogs and start waking up these silly humans."

He turned around and pointed at the empty corner where the band had been. For a moment, no one spoke. Then he spun back to face them. His eyes were slits of rage.

"Sort out the decorations and find me

some music," he hissed. "And give me that piñata. I'll use it to create the best party games ever."

One of the real goblins pulled a pumpkin-shaped piñata out from under his cloak. It was glowing purple. Paula gasped and nudged Rachel and Kirsty.

"That's my petrifying piñata!" she whispered.

Jack Frost snatched it and strode towards the door.

"We have to stop him!" whispered Paula.

He had reached the door . . . she waved her wand . . .

"BOO!" shouted the pumpkin piñata into Jack Frost's face.

A spooky carved face had had appeared
on the piñata.

The result was electrifying. Jack Frost
screamed and flung the piñata back over
his head. It hit one of the real goblins
and he fell over backwards, clutching it.

"BOO!" shouted the piñata again.

The goblin squawked and flung it away
from him – straight into Rachel's arms.

She immediately threw it to Paula.

"Yes!" Kirsty exclaimed.

"This isn't a game of catch," Jack Frost snapped.

Then Paula took off her mask.

Jack Frost let out a roar of rage. Blue lightning crackled all around him.

"Catch her!" he shrieked, as Rachel and Kirsty pulled off their masks. "Catch them all!"

Chapter Fifteen
Happy Halloween, Jack Frost!

Rachel and Kirsty looked around for an exit, but Paula did not move. Instead, she smiled at Jack Frost.

"I remember what Trixie said about you last Halloween," she said.

"Shut up!" Jack Frost shouted.

"She said you had *fun*," Paula went on.

Rachel and Kirsty stared at him in surprise. He actually looked embarrassed.

"I think you must really love Halloween to want to have all the pumpkin fun here at the castle," said Paula in a kind voice. "But the thing is, there is plenty of fun to go around. You don't have to steal it."

Jack Frost stopped shouting.

"I will decorate your Halloween ball," Paula promised. "I'll create amazing games and delicious food. I know some amazing pumpkin recipes. But you have to stop trying to spoil the holiday for everyone else."

Jack Frost wasn't scowling any more. His eyes opened wide and he nodded.

"I just want to have a happy Halloween," he mumbled.

The fairies shared an amazed glance. Then Paula raised her wand.

Wave after wave of pumpkin-shaped sparkles tumbled across the ballroom. It glowed with fairy magic as it was transformed into a spooky wonderland. Gossamer-thin cobwebs glimmered in every corner. Real candles flickered in thousands of tiny jack-o'-lanterns. Round tables, draped in purple velvet, were laden with golden plates of pumpkin pies, gingerbread men, pumpkin muffins, pumpkin tarts and pumpkin pasties,

with goblets of spiced hot chocolate and
meringue puffs filled with sweet pumpkin
cream. The dance floor gleamed, and
magical music echoed through the halls
of the castle.

"Happy Halloween, Jack Frost," said Paula.

He gazed around in wonder.

"I want everyone to see this," he said.

"Shall I send a magical invitation to all the fairies?" Paula asked.

Jack Frost nodded, and Rachel and Kirsty looked at each other in astonishment.

"How strange," said Kirsty. "The spookiest festival of the year seems to make Jack Frost nicer!"

Soon, fairies were fluttering into the ballroom, amazed to have been invited. Jack Frost welcomed them with a bow, and the goblins served glasses of pumpkin cordial and spiced blackberry juice. Trixie arrived and flew over to hug Paula, Rachel and Kirsty.

"I knew that you would help make things right," she said, smiling. "It's great to see you again."

"You too," said Rachel. "Happy Halloween!"

"This is the best Halloween yet," Paula said. "Thank you both for all your help. Now it's time for you to go and enjoy your own party."

She tapped their lockets with her wand, filling them with fairy dust again. Then the ballroom began to fade. The last thing the girls saw before it vanished was Jack Frost asking Paula to dance.

Moments later, the girls were sitting behind the straw bales at Pumpkin Patch Farm. The Harvesters were standing a few steps away.

"I feel a bit dizzy," said the lead singer.

"Me too," said the drummer. "Let's go back in. I've just had an amazing idea for a song about a spooky castle."

Giggling, Rachel and Kirsty followed the band into the barn. The first thing they saw was Polly cuddling the stray dog that had helped them earlier. She looked up at the girls, and her eyes shone with happiness.

"Dad says I can keep her," she told them.

"That's brilliant," said Kirsty. "Happy Halloween, Polly."

"Happy Halloween," said Polly, smiling. "I think I'm going to love Wetherbury after all!"

The End

Now it's time for Kirsty and
Rachel to help ...

Soraya the Skiing Fairy

Read on for a sneak peek ...

It was early morning in the Mistfall
Mountains. The rising sun beamed down
on a large wooden chalet at the edge
of a snowy pine forest. Shafts of sunlight
pierced the gaps in the curtains.

Kirsty Tate sat up in bed, rubbing her
eyes.

"Even the morning light looks different
here," she said.

Her best friend, Rachel Walker, leaned
over the edge of the top bunk and smiled
down at her.

"Mum says that Dewbelle is the

prettiest resort in Silverlake Valley," she said. "She worked here when she was a teenager."

Kirsty threw back her thick quilt and Rachel half-jumped down the bunk-bed ladder. Together, they pulled back the curtains and flung open the window. A cold, crisp scent filled the little room. Outside, the freshly fallen snow looked as smooth as icing. It had been dark when they had arrived the night before. Now they could see far beyond the ski slopes of Dewbelle, to where the Mistfall Mountains rose in the distance.

"The snow looks perfect," said Kirsty. "We could build a million snowmen."

Rachel laughed.

"We're going to be too busy learning how to ski," she said. "I can't wait to get started. I just hope that Jack Frost doesn't spoil the fun."

It was six months since the summer Gold Medal Games, when lots of children from different schools had come together to learn how to surf and skateboard. Now it was time for the winter games. Kirsty gazed at the ski slopes in silence.

"Are you OK?" asked Rachel, giving her a friendly nudge.

"I can't help thinking about what Jack Frost said in the summer," Kirsty replied. "He said that winter was *his* time. He's had months to plan something really horrible."

During the summer competition, Rachel and Kirsty had shared a wonderful adventure. Jack Frost had stolen the magical items that belonged to

the Gold Medal Fairies. Calling himself
Lightning Jack of the Frost Academy,
he had tried to win the competitions by
cheating. Rachel and Kirsty had helped
to foil his plans, but he still had two of
the magical items.

"He's never defeated the fairies, and
he never will," said Rachel. "Let's go
and have breakfast. This mountain air is
making me hungry."

All the competitors were staying in the
same chalet. As soon as they were dressed
they hurried down the wooden stairs.
Two boys and a girl joined them on the
way, and Rachel and Kirsty introduced
themselves.

"I'm Valentina," said the girl. "This is
Lenny . . ."

"And I'm Lee Vee," said the blond boy.

"This place is amazing, isn't it? I can't wait to try snowboarding."

"Be patient, we're learning to ski first," said Valentina, grinning.

Read **Soraya the Skiing Fairy** to find out what adventures are in store for Kirsty and Rachel!

Calling all parents, carers and teachers!
The Rainbow Magic fairies are here to help
your child enter the magical world of reading.
Whatever reading stage they are at, there's
a Rainbow Magic book for everyone!
Here is Lydia the Reading Fairy's guide to
supporting your child's journey at all levels.

Starting Out
Our Rainbow Magic Beginner Readers are perfect for first-time readers who are just beginning to develop reading skills and confidence. Approved by teachers, they contain a full range of educational levelling, as well as lively full-colour illustrations.

Developing Readers
Rainbow Magic Early Readers contain longer stories and wider vocabulary for building stamina and growing confidence. These are adaptations of our most popular Rainbow Magic stories, specially developed for younger readers in conjunction with an Early Years reading consultant, with full-colour illustrations.

Going Solo
The Rainbow Magic chapter books – a mixture of series and one-off specials – contain accessible writing to encourage your child to venture into reading independently. These highly collectible and much-loved magical stories inspire a love of reading to last a lifetime.

www.orchardseriesbooks.co.uk

"Rainbow Magic got my daughter reading chapter books. Great sparkly covers, cute fairies and traditional stories full of magic that she found impossible to put down" - Mother of Edie (6 years)

"Florence LOVES the Rainbow Magic books. She really enjoys reading now" - Mother of Florence (6 years)

Read along the Reading Rainbow!

Well done – you have completed the book!

This book was worth 2 stars.

See how far you have climbed on the Reading Rainbow opposite.
The more books you read, the more stars you can colour in
and the closer you will be to becoming a Royal Fairy!

Do you want to print your own Reading Rainbow?

1) Go to the Rainbow Magic website

2) Download and print out the poster

3) Colour in a star for every book you finish
and climb the Reading Rainbow

4) For every step up the rainbow,
you can download your very own certificate

There's all this and lots more at
orchardseriesbooks.co.uk

You'll find activities, stories, a special newsletter
AND you can search for the fairy with your name!